SPIKE'S
BEST NEST

First edition for the United States, Canada,
and the Philippines published 1997 by
Barron's Educational Series, Inc.

First published 1997 by Piccadilly Press Ltd.
London, England

All inquiries should be addressed to:
Barron's Educational Series, Inc.
250 Wireless Boulevard
Hauppauge, New York 11788

International Standard Book No. 0-7641-0548-5

Library of Congress Catalog Card No. 97-40812

Library of Congress Cataloging-in-Publication Data

Maddox, Tony.
    Spike's best nest / Tony Maddox. — 1st ed.
        p.   cm.
        Summary: Thinking that he would be happier living someplace new,
Spike the sparrow tries out several other animals' homes before
deciding that his old nest is the best for him.
        ISBN 0-7641-0548-5
        [1. Sparrows—Fiction.   2. Animals—Habitations—Fiction.]
    I. Title.
    PZ7.M25647Sr   1998   97-40812
                                                                                CIP
                                                                                AC

PRINTED IN BELGIUM
9 8 7 6 5 4 3 2 1

Tony Maddox lives in Worcestershire, England. Barron's is the American publisher
of his tremendously successful books, *Fergus the Farmyard Dog, Fergus's Big Splash,* and
Fergus's Upside-Down Day.

SPIKE'S BEST NEST

Tony Maddox

One morning Spike woke up
feeling really grumpy.
He looked around and sighed.
"I'm bored with this old nest.
It's time I found somewhere
better to live."

He went to tell Wise Owl.
"I want to find a new place to live,"
he said, "so I won't feel so grumpy."

"Why not come and live with me?"
said Wise Owl. Spike was delighted.
"What a good idea!" he said.

That evening, Spike settled down to sleep in
Wise Owl's nest. Just as he closed his eyes
he heard, "Too-wit, Too-woo. Too-wit, Too-woo."

He looked out to see Wise Owl singing to the moon. "I'll never get any sleep here!" he groaned.

Feeling very tired, Spike set off
early next morning to find
somewhere new to live. At the
farmyard, Mother Hen said,
"Stay with me in the hen house."

But Spike wasn't very happy when
she left him to baby-sit her eggs!

"Come live with us, Spike," said Freddie Fieldmouse and he pointed to the ragged scarecrow that stood in the big cornfield.

But Freddie had
a very large family!

He went to the grassy hill where
the rabbits played. "Come and
share our burrow, Spike!" they said.

But when Spike peered into
the rabbit burrow, he saw it
was much too dark and gloomy.

The day was almost over when
he met the three green frogs.
"Come with us, Spike," they croaked.
"We know just the place for your new nest!"

They took him to their pond
and pointed to the lily pads.
"Choose any one you like," they said.

When nighttime came,
Spike sat shivering on a
lily pad. It was cold and dark
and he felt very miserable.
Around him the frogs slept soundly.
He thought about his old nest
and how warm and cozy it had been.
He knew there was only one thing to do!

Later that night, Wise Owl flew by
Spike's old nest. He was surprised
to see someone asleep there.

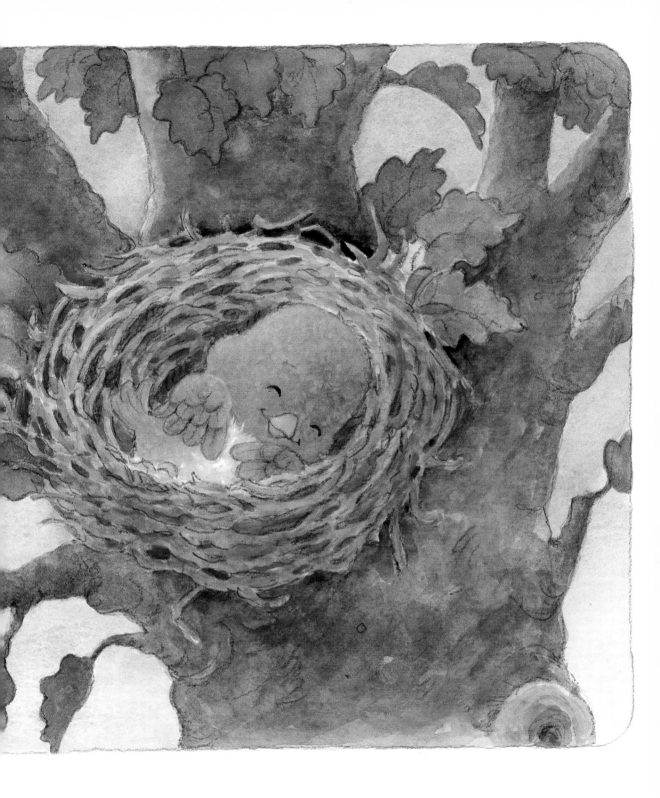

When he looked closer he saw
it was...Spike!

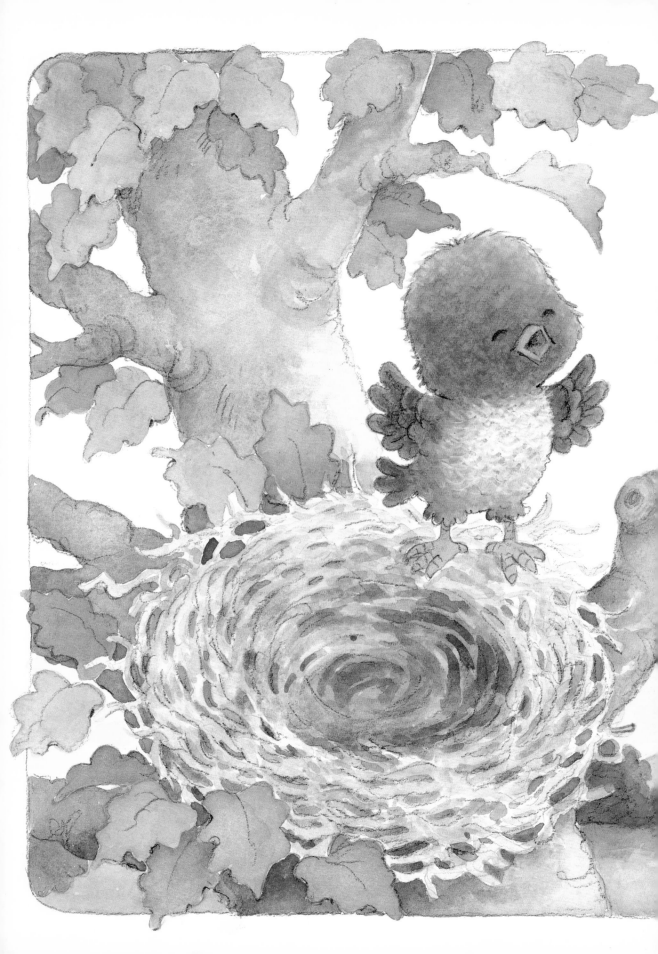

When Spike woke up the next morning, he didn't feel grumpy any more. His nest was the best nest after all! And he sang the happiest song he knew.

The End